FRIENDS
OF ACPL

THE
APPRENTICE
AND THE
PRIZE

THE
APPRENTICE
AND THE
PRIZE

WRITTEN AND ILLUSTRATED BY

Janice Holland

THE VANGUARD PRESS, INC.
New York

Designed by Betty Crumley

Library of Congress Catalogue Card Number: 58–13677

Manufactured in the United States of America

To My Mother

1055413

CARLO CARRARI stopped to drink at the Fountain of the Angels, just around the corner from Maestro Verner Doni's studio. The sundial on the wall told him that it was only a few moments before eight o'clock. Probably the Maestro's other apprentices were already putting on their leather aprons and beginning their various tasks.

Bredo was no doubt mixing the gesso, or plaster, with which to prepare the carved wooden figures for painting. Marco and Pietro always sharpened the carver's tools, and Giorgio opened the jars of color. Carlo, who was often the first to arrive, sometimes ground new colors for the Maestro. At other times he went to fetch oil, or the eggs whose yolks were used in mixing the paints.

This morning, however, Carlo hung over the fountain. Slowly he trailed his fingers in the green water, shattering the lacework of light that lay at the bottom of the pool. If only there were some good excuse for not going to the studio at all today!

7

He plunged one arm into the pool up to the elbow. Not only was no excuse possible, but now, more than ever, Maestro Doni needed all his apprentices, for his great carving for the high altar of the Church of Santa Maria must be ready by Saturday, and there was still much to be done.

The clock in the Piazza Grande began to strike the hour. For a moment Carlo listened. Then, swallowing hard, he bolted around the corner and up the stairs to the studio.

Quickly and quietly as a shadow, he slipped into the room, fastened on his apron, and got out his brushes. Carlo glanced about the studio, hoping desperately that Maestro Doni had already arrived. The light shimmering across the wet paint on the mixing slabs caught his eye. But the statue of Saint John the Baptist, which the Maestro was now carving, was still covered as for the night. No, the Maestro was not yet here. Though the sunlight, falling from the high windows, bathed him in warmth, Carlo shivered.

There was one thing to be thankful for, anyway. The other boys were already at their places before the carving. They were chattering so excitedly about the great pageant that only the night before had wound through the streets of Assisi, that they scarcely noticed Carlo's arrival.

Without a sound he hunted out the pot of rose madder. He went to the center of the carving and knelt before the figure of the Virgin. For the past two days Carlo had worked with great care upon the delicate rose and silver design that bordered her robe. Today he would finish it.

8

For some time the other boys continued to exclaim over the pageant. The great celebration of the three-hundredth year since the birth of Saint Francis was the most glorious the city had ever held in honor of her native son. Its beauty had not been lost upon the young artists in Maestro Doni's studio.

"The torches carried by the friars looked like a river of fire!" said Giorgio.

"And the flowing robes of the cardinals—they glowed like red wine in the night!" added Marco.

Convinced at last that they had forgotten him, Carlo was just beginning to lose himself in the joy of his painting when Pietro's voice jerked him back to reality.

"Where were you last night, Carlo? I didn't catch so much as a glimpse of you. And you haven't had a word to say this morning."

Carlo did not answer at once. He hoped Pietro would soon turn to something else, but there was an awkward silence while the boy stood watching him with questioning eyes.

"Oh, I went over to Mount Subasio to see the sunset. Something happened, and I couldn't get back on time."

Pietro stared at Carlo. "Are you crazy? It's once in a hundred years that Assisi celebrates the birth of Saint Francis as she did last night. You and I won't even be alive the next time it comes around. And you couldn't be bothered to see it!"

Carlo said nothing. He only dipped his brush more hurriedly into the pot of rose madder.

"That's right!" Giorgio chimed in. "I remember wondering myself where you were. Father Giovanni will be furious with you for not attending Mass! Everyone in Assisi, and all the folk for miles around, were there. Some even came from Rome. What kept you on Subasio, anyway?"

"Hey! Watch what you're doing, Giorgio! You nearly spilled that ultramarine down my neck!" shouted the tall, handsome Bredo as he smoothed off the tip of an angel's nose. Then he left his place and walked half the length of the carving, until he stood at the center, behind Carlo.

"Come on, little one! Tell us your secret! What kept you on Mount Subasio while all Assisi was celebrating?"

Carlo bent closer over the hem of the Virgin's robe. He could feel a hot flush spreading over his face. He knew Bredo was looking down on him with the mocking smile that so often came to his lips. Bredo was so handsome, so sure of himself, and such a skillful carver! He seemed to have only contempt for ordinary people.

"Maybe you saw a vision of Saint Francis himself? And Saint Clare, and all the angels of Heaven?" Bredo suggested. "Surely nothing less would have kept you from Mass?"

By this time the other boys had gathered to watch the show. Bredo decided to make it a good one.

"Look at him!" He bent over Carlo, who by now was attending even more closely to his painting. "It's certain he's thin enough to melt away and be an angel himself, with that fine golden hair of his!"

10

He poked Carlo in the ribs. "I've heard that if you don't eat regularly, it's much easier to see visions!" Bredo went on. "When did you eat last?"

Giorgio, Marco, and Pietro snickered. Bredo was so clever. Since he had such a proud way with him, it was most flattering that he seemed just now to be taking them into his confidence. Still, there was something that made one afraid of him, too.

Bredo put his palms together in mock holiness and looked up toward Heaven. "Oh, Saint Francis! And all the other saints! . . ." But suddenly his hands dropped to his sides, and a charming smile flashed across his face.

"Ah! Maestro Doni! We were all trying to help Carlo with his colors here. Don't you think he has the red a little too bright along the hem?"

Carlo drew a deep breath as he straightened up and turned around. Good Maestro Doni! There he stood, with the kindly wrinkles lining his cheeks and brow. He looked at Bredo for several seconds without speaking, and his face had a sternness rarely seen.

"No," Maestro Doni said very quietly. "Carlo has an excellent sense of color. He really does not need your advice."

For a moment Bredo seemed about to defy the Maestro. The other boys crept silently back to their work on the carving. At last Bredo, too, returned to his place.

Carlo wondered. Whenever the Maestro appeared, Bredo

always assumed his charming, aristocratic ways. Did the Maestro suspect that he was sometimes quite otherwise?

Maestro Doni looked carefully at the boys' work. Yes, everything was progressing beautifully. All these apprentices were uncommonly gifted. Carlo and Bredo were really outstanding. Within a few days the great carving would be ready for its journey to Rome.

"What shall we be working on next, Maestro?" the boys wanted to know. "Will it be the figure of Saint John that you have been carving these past few weeks?"

Maestro Doni smiled quizzically. "It is something you will like better than that," he said. "You will each be working on a figure of your own!"

"Oh?" There was an excited hush as the boys waited for the Maestro to continue.

"As you know, this is the three-hundredth year since the good Saint Francis was born here in Assisi. The city magistrates have decided to commemorate his birth by offering a prize of six hundred ducats for a statue of the Saint. This statue must have the very spirit of the good friar himself. It will be chosen by the magistrates, with the help of Pierre le Bris, the noted French sculptor. The competition is open to anyone in Italy."

At first the boys shouted with excitement. "Six hundred ducats!" Why, one could visit Rome, France, and Germany with that! One could probably see all the great art works of Europe with six hundred ducats!

Then Carlo spoke timidly. "Surely, Maestro Doni, you will wish to make a figure of Saint Francis yourself. And you will win the prize, for you are the greatest sculptor in Italy!"

Maestro Doni smiled and shook his head. "No," he said, "I already have more work than I can do. Besides, Saint Francis is the Saint of youth. More than any other, he had the joy of everlasting springtime. It would not be fitting for an old man like me to carve the figure of Saint Francis."

Carlo was still doubtful. "What of the other great sculptors, like Maestro Verrocchio?" he asked.

"I think you need not fear competition from them. The prize is not really large enough to attract the masters. You are all very talented boys. You have had good, thorough training here with me. Your chances of winning are equal to those of anyone in Italy.

"Between now and next Thursday, I want each of you to learn all you can about Saint Francis. Then surrender your spirit to the spirit of the good Saint. One cannot give to a work of art what he does not have in himself. On Thursday morning you will show me your designs and tell me what you hope to express in your statues of Saint Francis."

That afternoon Carlo hurried down the narrow Via Fonte Marcella to the bakery where his friend Antonio worked.

Antonio was just removing a large pan of rolls from the great brick oven. His face brightened as Carlo entered.

"Carlo! What in the world happened to you last night? I hunted for you all evening!"

"I'll tell you in a moment, but first you must hear the news! Today Maestro Doni announced that on the last of May a prize will be given for the best statue of Saint Francis. He wants us all to try. Just think! Six hundred ducats for a single figure!"

"What in the world would you do with all that money?" Antonio asked, wide-eyed.

"Oh, I'd go to Rome and see the great buildings and statues there. Maybe I'd even go to France and Germany. A sculptor has to study the works of the masters, and I . . . I've never been out of Assisi."

For a moment Carlo seemed lost in happy thoughts. Then a shadow crossed his face. "Antonio, will you come with me to Mount Subasio? I must do something there at once."

"Well, yes. We're through with the baking now, and Pappa won't care if I leave. But what must you do on Mount Subasio?"

"I'll tell you as we go. Let's get started."

Quickly the boys set off down the Via Fonte Marcella. At every gap and turn, the misty blue hills surrounding Assisi could be seen. Carlo was talking so excitedly that the ragged children, who were everywhere along the streets, tittered as he passed.

16

The two boys only hurried along the faster over the rough, cobbled pavements. Down, down, they wound their way, past the narrow little stone and stucco houses clinging desperately to the hillsides. Carlo's words tumbled over themselves in his eagerness to tell Antonio why he was going to Mount Subasio.

"You remember, I said yesterday that I was going over to the mountain to watch the sunset? Well, I had almost reached the top when I heard a noise—just a little one—in a nearby thicket. As I pushed aside the bushes, I saw a half-grown fawn. It looked at me with such sorrowful eyes that I was afraid it had been hurt, but I could not quite tell, for its legs were doubled under it, and it was a little too large for me to lift. How I wished then that I were big and strong, like Bredo!"

"If you'd been Bredo, you'd probably have killed it," Antonio said sharply.

Carlo shrugged his shoulders. "Maybe," he said, "but I don't believe even Bredo would have had the heart to hurt it. It seemed so hungry and weak. I hurried down to a nearby farm, where they gave me a little milk. Twice I had to return for more.

"The little thing drank as though it were starved, and when I turned to leave, it looked at me with those great, sad eyes, and made little soft sounds, as though it were weeping. I was afraid some wild animal would find it during the night, so I stayed on with it as long as I dared."

"So that's why you weren't at the pageant!" Antonio exclaimed. "You missed the most wonderful procession Assisi has ever seen—and you an artist, too. It's really a pity, though it's certain Saint Francis himself would have done the same."

But Carlo's thoughts were still with the fawn. "All day I've been worrying about it," he said. "If it is still in the thicket, it will be terribly hungry by now—and lonely, too. That's why I want to stop at the farm for some more milk today."

While they were talking, the boys had crossed the valley and begun the gentle climb up the mountain. It was April, and the chestnut woods were veiled in tender green. Already the valley had fallen into shadow, but as Carlo and Antonio reached the higher part of the mount, shafts of light pierced the green wood like golden arrows.

Soon a little clearing appeared, with a single small cottage at its center. Through the cottage roof came a curl of smoke.

"There's Signora Coletti's farm," Carlo said. "Today I have some money, and I can pay her for the milk she gave me yesterday, as well as buying more."

"*Buon giorno!*" called Signora Coletti, wiping her hands on her apron as she came around the corner of the cottage. "Ah, *sì*—here is that sweet lad who cares so for the little fawn! And this is your friend? Ah, *sì*! Perhaps he is like you? I hope so!"

Carlo reached into his pocket for a dinaro, which he handed to the Signora. "This is for the milk I got yesterday, and please, may I have another flagon now?"

Signora Coletti counted out the change from the pouch that hung from her waist. "The flask today—is it for the little one?" she asked. "Or is it for yourself?"

"Oh, it's for the fawn, of course. I just hope the little creature is still there, and that no harm has come to it through the night," Carlo answered quickly.

The Signora's good, strong face broke into a bright smile. "Come with me," she said. Carlo and Antonio followed her around to the back of the cottage, where there was a rough shed. This was the home of Tessa, the cow. There she stood, swinging her tail and silently chewing her cud.

Just beyond her, in the dark corner, Carlo could dimly see another form. Could it be . . . He hurried closer.

"Oh, Signora! You have brought him here!" And in a trice Carlo was on his knees, with his arms around the fawn and his thin little face close against its head.

"*Sì, sì*. When my Giuseppe came home, after you had gone, I told him all that had happened. My Giuseppe is like you. He loves everything that lives, he does. He said the fawn must never stay alone in those woods all night. So he lit a torch and went up the mountain, following your footprints in the soft clay of the road. How happy I was when I saw him coming with the little one in his arms!" The Signora gently patted the creature's graceful head.

"Is the little fellow hurt?" Carlo asked, feeling the fawn's legs. "Or was he just frightened almost to death?"

"My Giuseppe says he is not hurt much. He has a little sprain, that is all. Soon he will be well again, and big enough to go into the forest alone. Then we will set him free."

"Oh, Signora," Carlo whispered happily, "you love the fawn as much as I do." He dug into his pocket again.

"Here, take the other dinaro. It's all I have, but it will help to pay for the milk and hay you will give him."

"No, no. Tessa will give her milk gladly for the little one! But by the saints, I believe you need food more than he does. Come with me into the cottage."

Carlo and Antonio followed Signora Coletti into the whitewashed kitchen. Over the fire in the center hung a copper kettle, chatting cozily with itself. A delicious odor of herbs and onions and freshly baked bread filled the room.

"Sit down," said the Signora, hastily clearing some embroidery work from the heavy wooden table by the window. "The walk back to Assisi is long. My Giuseppe will be late again tonight. You must have supper here with me, and then I will not be so lonely!"

Over the steaming goodness of the thick soup and soft bread, Signora Coletti questioned the boys. "So you both live in Assisi, eh? You are Carlo Carrari? Is it your father who has the fruit shop in the Via Fonte Marcella?"

Carlo's face lit up. "You know my father?" he asked.

"Ah, sì, sì! Many times he has bought the fruit that Giuseppe and I have grown in our orchard here. But I have never seen you in the shop. How is that?"

Carlo felt the reproach in the Signora's tone. He had often been told that the son of a poor fruiterer should never try to become a sculptor. He was too ambitious. Now, under the Signora's questioning gaze, he felt this must be true.

"Well, you see . . ." Carlo did not know quite how to explain what was in his heart.

"Carlo's going to be a sculptor," Antonio said quickly. "He and I have been friends all our lives. Carlo has to be a sculptor because he is miserable unless he is carving or drawing. He has been at it ever since I can remember. And when Signor Carrari showed his work to Maestro Doni, the Maestro said he would gladly take Carlo into his studio as an apprentice." Antonio looked proudly at his friend. "The most talented boys in Italy all try to get into Maestro Doni's studio, and the Maestro takes so very few. It is a great honor to be an apprentice there."

Signora Coletti looked at Carlo with new admiration. "Ah, I knew you were no ordinary lad," she said. "Not a boy in a hundred would have cared for that fawn as you did. Not when a fawn skin can be sold for three dinari—and you a poor lad, at that." For Carlo's faded vermilion jacket and worn shoes had already told her their story.

"Oh, we aren't really poor," Carlo said quickly. "It's just that while I'm an apprentice I have no extra time, and so my father has to hire another boy to help him in the shop. That is, since my mother died two winters ago, for she was always there with him, except while I was very small."

23

Before long Carlo found himself telling the Signora every-thing. She, like Antonio, would not laugh at him for the way he felt about animals—about little rabbits and kittens and birds.

"It's the look in their eyes," he said. "Surely it is the love of God himself that shines in the eyes of all little, innocent things. It is as though they were saying: 'I have nothing to give but love, and nothing to save me from those who are cruel. Though I cannot speak, I can feel the same joy and pain that are yours. Be kind, you who are strong, be kind.' "

"You sound like the good Saint Francis himself," said the Signora, looking at Carlo tenderly.

"Carlo's going to carve a statue of Saint Francis and win six hundred ducats!" Antonio said eagerly.

"Oh, Antonio, sculptors from all over Italy will be trying for that prize. How can you tell the Signora I will win?" Carlo's voice was stern, but his smile showed the warmth of his feeling for Antonio.

"Surely there can be no one more like the good Saint than yourself in this love for animals and birds," said Signora Coletti. "When will the prize be given?"

"The last of May," Carlo answered.

"Faith, then. Every day I shall light a candle and pray to Saint Francis to bless your statue with his very own spirit, so that you may win the prize."

"Oh, Signora, will you?" Carlo's grateful look said more than many words.

"You may depend upon it," she said, clasping his hand in hers. "And Giuseppe will join me. You must come to see us often, and Antonio must come with you." With her other hand she took one of Antonio's.

"But see now, it is almost dark. You must hurry, or you will not be able to find your way to Assisi without a great deal of trouble."

Antonio and Carlo said very little to each other as they walked home through the spring evening. Above Assisi the towers of Castle Rocco made a jagged line against the sunset. Below the castle the little clusters of houses roosting along the hillside looked like sleepy doves in the twilight. The murmuring waters of the Tescio soothed the valley, and smoke from the kitchen fires sweetened the air.

Carlo gave a happy little sigh. The pointed cypress trees that accented the hillsides seemed to be reaching upward— ever upward to the skies. They never really touched them, but the trying somehow made them very beautiful. Perhaps longing and love and trying would lend beauty to his statue of Saint Francis.

Just then the boys turned into the steep Via Portica, and Carlo, starting to run, shouted back to Antonio. "Beat you up the hill and home!" he said. Tonight, it seemed, his feet had wings.

THE MAESTRO had given the boys a week in which to design their statues. It flew like the wind for Carlo. One after another he sketched out his ideas for the figure, and one after another he crumpled them up in despair.

Over and over, from his mother's lips, he had heard the beautiful legends of the good friar. Carlo always liked to think of Saint Francis as walking the dusty roads, singing aloud to the wide skies his joy in the love of God and all that God had made.

Most saints were rather sorrowful—at least they looked so in the paintings that filled the churches. But Saint Francis said that joy was most pleasing to God—and truly, if one loved the sun and the moon, the wolf, the deer, and the birds, and even the air itself, as Saint Francis did, how could he be otherwise than happy? Saint Francis always spoke of "My Brother Fire" or "My Brother Sun," for to him all things were made by God his Father, so were they not indeed his brothers?

How could one ever capture such a living spirit in the silence of wood and paint? In sculpture there were form and color. With these alone the statue must be made to sing, to breathe. But the good Saint Francis was said to have been a frail man, whom one might never have noticed at all.

If only he had worn a brocaded cloak! Then there would have been something to ornament the figure. Instead, he had chosen the coarse brown robe in which his followers, the Franciscan friars, were even now seen on the streets of Assisi. No, there was no outer beauty to portray. All the glory of Saint Francis was in his golden spirit. Unless one could capture that, the statue would be dead.

On Wednesday afternoon Carlo took the winding road from Assisi to the Portiuncula, the little church where Saint Francis and his followers had so often gone to pray. Perhaps if he prayed there he, too, would feel the spirit of the good Saint and could put it into his work.

After making his devotions in the chapel, Carlo wandered into the little garden just outside. There grew the thornless roses, brought into being by the miraculous holiness of the Saint.

Carlo sat down on a stone bench and looked at the bare stalks standing in the hard brown earth. How forbidding they seemed now! Yet in a few weeks the miracle of spring would crown them with glorious blooms. . . . He jumped to his feet.

That was it! The fragrant flowers, springing from the hard, brown earth, were like the spirit of Saint Francis, springing from the plain figure in the coarse brown robe! At last Carlo knew how he wanted to carve his statue. He would show the friar with his head raised in joyous song, his robes flowing with life, and in his arms the thornless roses, the glory of his soul. Carlo hurried back to the studio. In the failing daylight he quickly sketched out the harmonious lines of his statue. So eagerly did he work that one piece of charcoal after another broke under his hand. Carlo scarcely noticed. His whole being was caught up in the ecstasy of the drawing.

When the daylight died he lit a candle, hardly knowing that he did so, and continued his work. He sketched the front, the two sides, and the back view of his statue. The clock in the Piazza Grande was chiming nine before he sat down, drew a deep and happy sigh, and snuffed out the light. His sketches were ready for the Maestro.

On Thursday morning Carlo arrived early, as usual. With small bits of wax he began to fasten his sketches to the wall at the rear of the studio. Before he had finished, Bredo came in. Then Giorgio and Pietro, and last of all, Marco. One after another they arranged their drawings on the wall below Carlo's. Just as they finished, Maestro Doni entered.

"Ah! I see you have all brought your designs," he said. His pleasure in the boys' enthusiasm for the contest was undisguised. One by one he studied the drawings. His apprentices watched him intently.

"This one is yours, Giorgio? Very good. Very good indeed. I see you have chosen to show Saint Francis as he preached to the birds."

"Yes, Maestro," Giorgio said quickly. "I hope to show in the good Saint's attitude his love for his 'little sisters, the birds.'"

"You have made a good beginning, but you must be careful to group the birds in such a way that your design will not be cluttered. You can easily do that, for the legend says the birds did not fly from Saint Francis even though he was so close as to touch them with his robe.

"And now, Pietro, you have evidently been attracted by Saint Francis' taming of the wolf of Gubbio."

"Yes. It seems to me most wonderful that after the wolf had terrorized all of Gubbio and killed several women and children, Saint Francis, speaking to it gently, so changed its nature that it became a great favorite in the town. I hope to show his compassion even for those who are fierce and cruel."

"I believe you will succeed, Pietro," the Maestro said. "Now, Marco, tell us what you have in mind."

"I wish to show Saint Francis when he met the young man who had caught many wild doves and was about to sell them in the market place. Saint Francis, you remember, persuaded the young man to give them to him. Then, holding them close to his bosom, he said, 'Oh, my little sisters, the doves, so simple, so innocent, and so chaste, why did you allow yourselves to be caught? I will save you from death, and make you nests, that you may increase and multiply, according to the command of God.' "

"That is an excellent choice, Marco, but you, like Giorgio, must be careful not to let the birds clutter your design. A statue must be simple, you know. A very great sculptor once said that every statute should be rolled downhill when it is finished, and anything that is broken off in the process should not have been there in the first place!" The Maestro's eyes twinkled.

"Well, Bredo, tell us now about your design."

"I have chosen no particular moment from the Saint's life," Bredo said. "What I wish to do is group the little animals and birds around him so as to express his love for them all. See, I have sketched in a squirrel, a rabbit, a pigeon, and several others, nestling against the folds in his robe."

"You are an excellent sculptor, Bredo. But you must not let your skill run away with you. A statue is not made better because of the number of things in it. Won't you try to simplify your design a little?"

Bredo was, as always, very polite to the Maestro. "I will try, sir," he said.

"And now, Carlo. I see you have a very simple design. That is good. Tell us about it."

"I have tried to make the figure as I thought Saint Francis himself would like it. It seemed to me that nothing could show his gentleness and his love like the beautiful thornless roses that I have put in his hands."

"Good, good," said the Maestro softly, almost as though to himself. Then he glanced around at his pupils. "I am well pleased with the way you have all begun your work. Now go into the storeroom and select for yourselves suitable blocks of walnut. You have no time to lose, for it is only seven weeks until the last of May, when the statues will be judged."

The boys rushed pell-mell through the door at the back of the studio and into the crowded, dusty storeroom. Wooden blocks of all shapes and sizes were stacked against the walls and scattered about the floor. Carlo poked in among them, looking for one with a smooth, even grain, and large enough for the standing figure with its flowing robes.

For a while the dust flew, as one boy after another moved blocks here and there, turned them over, and tapped them to be sure they were firm and solid.

Carlo was the last to make his choice, but finally he found a block that satisfied him. He carried it into the studio and bolted it to a stand. For a moment he stood looking at the beautiful, unmarked block. Sometimes he felt that no statue was ever so fair as the uncarved wood, with its fine grain flowing in swirling patterns. Now, before a single cut had marred it, all things beautiful were possible. If the hand that

32

shaped it were great enough, this block would make a master-
piece.

"Oh, good Saint Francis," Carlo said in a low voice, "in
you alone dwells the spirit that will make this statue live.
Please come to me and guide my hand." He paused a moment, as though he almost expected to hear the Saint give
answer. Then, trembling with excitement, he picked up his
chalk and began to trace the outline of his design upon the
wood.

For the next few weeks the studio hummed with the happy
sound of chisel and mallet. Chips of wood littered the floor,
and the rough outlines of the various figures began to ap-
pear. There was little of the usual banter and teasing among
the boys. Their eagerness to win the prize kept each at work
with an uncommon fury. The air seemed to crackle with ten-
sion. So constantly did they labor that Maestro Doni would
occasionally come into the room and say, "All right, boys!
Industry is a good thing, but one cannot create a work of
art by will power. Out with you! Go into the spring
sunlight and forget your carving. Let the sweetness of
the Umbrian April sink into your souls. That is the
stuff of which art is made." And so saying, the kindly
old sculptor would open the door and almost push the boys
through it.

On one such day, Carlo went to Mount Subasio and talked with Signora Coletti. Though the fawn had been set free some time before, Carlo loved to visit his new-found friend.

"*Sì, sì,*" the Signora said. "I know just what the Maestro means. One must prepare the soul to hear the harmonies of heaven, or he will have nothing in his heart to give. While one is so busy, one cannot listen."

To Carlo, this was a hard saying. His pulses literally throbbed with the longing to be back again at his work. But as the Signora talked, he began to feel the sweetness of the rain-washed air. The fever of ambition cooled within him, and a strange peace took its place.

"Ah, Signora, you are wise. You know the heart of the artist. How can that be, when you have never tried to paint or carve?"

"One cannot live, as I do, on the bosom of the earth without learning some of life's secrets. As you know, my Giuseppe is often away in the villages, selling our vegetables and fruits. Sometimes when I am alone I go to the top of the mountain and rest.

"From such a height I can see the towns: Assisi, Spello, and Foligno. Far below me the tired peasants with their oxcarts plod the dusty roads. The coaches of rich nobles dash from castle to castle, and the hunters ride to the forests with falcons on their wrists. But I am so far away that the noise and the dust do not reach me.

35

"Sometimes I think the world soils the spirits of men, as the dust of the road soils their bodies. It is then that they must climb the Mount Subasio of the soul, and listen to the voice of God."

Carlo looked at the Signora with shining eyes, for she seemed to know his inmost thoughts. As he turned to leave he said, "Signora, I cannot tell you all that I feel. Not since my mother died have I been so happy!"

The Signora smiled. "You have brought me something, too, you know. For I have never had a son, but if I had, I should have wished him such a lad as you. Good-by now, Carlo. And remember, I pray for you every night, that the spirit of Saint Francis may bless your work."

Next morning Carlo was at the studio as soon as it was light. As he let himself in the door, he was surprised to hear the tap of a mallet. It was the first time he had come so early, and he was hoping to work alone for a while before anyone else arrived.

It was Bredo who was there before him. Carlo had noticed that Bredo's work was progressing faster than that of any of the others, but had thought it due to his exceptional skill as a carver.

Bredo took no notice of Carlo's arrival, but went on furiously chipping and scraping at his figure. Carlo hardly felt offended, for Bredo, whose father was the richest merchant in Umbria, had made it plain long before that the son of a poor fruiterer was of no interest to him.

Carlo took out his tools and started toward the grind-stone to sharpen them. As he passed Bredo, he saw something that pierced his heart like a knife.

Bredo, ambitious and clever as he was, had a living model to work from. A brown rabbit, half grown, stood on its haunches on the table before him. It stood, because it could not move. For Bredo had taken the heavy wire sometimes used to support linen draperies, and bound the rabbit into position with it.

The terror in the poor dumb creature's eyes called out to Carlo for help. Without an instant's hesitation he started toward it. "Oh, Bredo, how could you—how could you?" he moaned.

"Keep away from that rabbit!" Bredo's voice was icy. "How do you suppose I've gotten such realism in my animals, anyway?"

"How can you carve a statue of Saint Francis, and in the carving torture the very creatures he loved?" Carlo asked.

"Who cares how I accomplish my carving?" Bredo answered. "My statue will last a hundred years or more. The wonderful, lifelike animals will be admired by everyone. What's the suffering of one little rabbit? The world is full of suffering."

"It is people like you who make it so!" breathed Carlo, his voice shaking with emotion. "Your cruelty will poison your art so that it were better you had never touched a chisel."

Bredo came toward him with upraised fist. "You little peasant!" he muttered between clenched teeth. "Who do you think you are, anyway? Saint Francis?"

Carlo felt in his pocket for a dinaro he had been saving toward the price of a new jacket. He held the coin out to Bredo. "Sell me the rabbit," he said. "You have almost finished your work on it, anyway."

For a moment Bredo remained in his threatening attitude. Then, with a sneer, he said, "Well! The poor fruiterer's son has so much money he can throw it around buying rabbits! Give me your dinaro—I've gotten the best use of the creature, anyway. Now take it and get out of here!"

Quickly Carlo unbound the rabbit. It was trembling with fright, and lame from the pressure of the wires. Tenderly he put it inside his jacket, next to his heart. He would take it to Signora Coletti. How wonderful to know that she would understand!

THE TEMPO of work in the studio heightened as the contest neared its close. Boiling glue filled the air with an acrid smell, for the boys mixed it with the gesso that they applied to their figures. Deep-blue stones of lapis lazuli were finely ground to make the beautiful color called ultramarine. Crystals of flaming cinnabar were powdered into pure vermilion red. Other stones and minerals were crushed into smooth blends of color on the mixing slabs of porphyry.

Maestro Doni often passed through the room, suggesting a change here, a refinement there, in one figure or another. If he had any favorite among them, he did not betray it by the slightest sign. He devoted himself to helping each lad to perfect his own idea.

The morning of the judging, all the figures were taken to the Piazza della Minerva. Carlo held his breath as he and old Guido Maffioli carried his figure down the stairs from the studio and placed it in Guido's oxcart. Carlo tenderly packed straw around it, lest the jogging of the cart on the uneven streets break off the least portion of the work. The Maestro might say that all statues should be rolled downhill, but Carlo was not going to try it with his!

As the figures were being set up around the square, the villagers stared in admiration. Besides the five from Maestro Doni's studio, there were eleven from other parts of Italy. Carlo could not help feeling secretly that none of the latter equaled those made by Maestro Doni's students. He looked at his own work. The sun was slanting across it so that the dazzling light caught the joyous smile on Saint Francis' upturned face. The brown robe below fell into shadow, but the light blazed again on the circlet of thornless roses, white as pearls, in his hands.

Carlo sighed. Whoever won the prize, he knew that this was the best carving he had ever done.

The judges were to begin their work at ten o'clock, and the prize was to be announced at four in the afternoon. When Carlo thought about it, his heart beat so hard that it almost choked him. If only he could win! Even more than the money, he wanted to show his neighbors in Assisi that the fruiterer's son had not dreamed idle dreams or let foolish ambition run away with him. If he won the prize he would have proved his worth as an artist. Nothing in the world seemed so important as that.

All day Carlo wandered about like one in a trance. When he thought of four o'clock and the announcement of the prize, his palms became moist and icy.

He went to the bakery to talk to Antonio. "By all the saints," said Antonio in a worried tone, "if you go on like this you'll faint dead away before four o'clock!"

By three o'clock Carlo felt as though two butter churns were working in the pit of his stomach. When the clock in the Piazza Grande chimed the quarter hour before four, Carlo started for the square. By the time he reached it, a crowd had already gathered. All of Assisi was waiting for the news of the award. Carlo stepped into the shadow of an arched doorway.

The balcony of the city hall had been decorated with brocaded velvet and flowers. The sculptor, Pierre le Bris, and the magistrates filed onto it and took their places one by one. From inside the arched windows behind them, strains of sacred music were heard. A solemn hush stole over the waiting people.

As soon as the clock finished striking four, the chief magistrate stepped forward and raised his hand.

"Friends, as you all know, we are gathered here to honor the sculptor whose statue has been judged the most fitting one by which Assisi may commemorate her beloved Saint Francis. The judges had a most difficult task in choosing a winner from among these excellent works. However, there is one which seemed to them to have extraordinary power and realism, particularly in the carving of the little animals so dear to our good Saint . . ."

Carlo blanched. It couldn't be . . .

"That is the statue carved by Signor Bredo Ugolino. Signor Ugolino has been awarded the prize. If the Signor is present, will he please come up here so that we may make the presentation?"

There was a great stir in the crowd, but Carlo hardly noticed it. His temples throbbed, his throat ached, he could hardly see. Bredo! Bredo had won! How was it possible?

Carlo turned quickly and fled from the square. He could not bear to see Bredo, with his false but charming smile, accepting the award. Without knowing where he was going, Carlo stumbled down the winding streets and out into the valley.

He would have gone to the Signora, but he could not bear to tell her that all her prayers had been in vain. Not yet, anyway. He knew she had always believed that he would win. How could he ever let her know what had happened?

Carlo had no idea how long he had been walking before he found himself at the door of Maestro Doni's studio. If only the Maestro were inside! Perhaps he could explain why this terrible thing had happened. Carlo lifted the latch and entered.

The sun had just dropped behind Castle Rocco, and the gloom of evening already filled the studio. The white coverings over some unfinished figures looked like ghosts in the twilight. There was an eerie stillness in the room. Then he heard the Maestro's voice: "Come in, Carlo. I have been waiting for you."

44

Carlo had not seen the Maestro, who was sitting quietly beside one of the great windows, looking across the city to the purple hills.

"Oh, Maestro . . ." Carlo could contain himself no longer. Great sobs shook his shoulders as he knelt before his teacher. "How could it have happened this way? Bredo does not even love the good Saint Francis. He tortured the little creatures he carved by wiring them into their poses!"

"I know, I know," the Maestro murmured, putting his hand softly upon Carlo's head. For some moments he said nothing more, but let Carlo sob out his agony until it began to ebb. Then he said, "This is a great disappointment to me, too, although I feared it might happen. Bredo's skill in carving is rare. But to find a boy who can give a statue the simple grace and gladness that your Saint Francis has is rarer by far. You must not despair because Bredo has won the prize. Sometimes it takes greatness to recognize greatness. The cleverness of Bredo's work is apparent to everyone, but cleverness soon becomes tiresome.

"There is another factor that may have influenced the decision. As you know, Bredo's father is very well to do. He has made rich gifts to Perugia and Spello. There is reason to believe he will do the same for Assisi. Though I know the magistrates would not admit, even to themselves, that this had anything to do with their choice, I cannot help believing it was so. Assisi is a poor town and needs all the money it can get."

Carlo looked up at his teacher. He had always admired and respected him, but the Maestro had seemed as far above him as a god. Now, as he looked into the deep, calm eyes and saw the twilight lingering on the silver hair and beard, he loved him as a friend.

"Many years ago," the Maestro continued, "I myself entered a similar competition. For weeks I labored, early and late, putting all my soul into my carving. With the prize went a commission to carve the altar screen for the most magnificent church in Florence. I wanted that opportunity more than I have ever wanted anything since. But the prize and the opportunity went to another. I knew he was unworthy of so sacred a trust, and for a time, at least, I almost lost my faith in God. I hated the whole world, for it seemed to be filled with injustice and cruelty. But one does not live for nothing. The long years since then have taught me many things. And one of the greatest is this: that he who loves is never the loser."

The Maestro stopped suddenly. "Which would you rather have," he asked, "the spirit of Saint Francis, or the six hundred ducats?"

Carlo realized what the Maestro wanted him to say. He knew that the Maestro was right, but just now he did not feel that anything could ever console him for the loss of the coveted prize.

"Surely you know the answer to that," he murmured, looking down at the floor.

The Maestro put his arm around his pupil.

"This is the pain of youth," he said. "But it will not always be so. No one can love as Saint Francis loved without learning that hope and love sometimes lose their way in sorrow. You are very like the good Saint, my lad, and the cruelty of the world will often make you weep. But that will not be the end. For Saint Francis found the joy that lies hidden beyond the pain . . . the joy that the world can never take away. Some day that joy will come to you. Go now, and remember, and wait for that joy."

Carlo gave his teacher a grateful look. He wanted to speak, to thank him for all he had said, but he could not find the words. With a shy smile he turned and slipped out into the night. The weeks and weeks of work had left him worn out. Joy was only a word—a faraway word. He groped his way home in the darkness and fell into bed.

Carlo remembered nothing more until the next morning, when he was awakened by a heavy pounding at his door, and shouts of "Carlo! Carlo!" It was Antonio's voice, but what in the world was the matter?

Still half asleep, Carlo opened the door.

"Come at once, Carlo! You must see! There is a crowd of people in the square, and they are all looking at your statue. Hurry!"

Carlo dressed hastily and followed Antonio. Arriving at the Piazza della Minerva, he saw men, women, and children standing before his statue. They were hushed and still. All were looking in the same direction. Carlo followed their gaze up, up to the figure. And there, in the hands of Saint Francis, among the thornless roses, a white dove sat upon her new-made nest.

"Surely the spirit of Saint Francis, who freed the captive doves, lives in that statue!" whispered an old woman nearby. "This dove feels that holy love, and knows she is safe in his arms!"

"A white dove!" murmured another, crossing herself. "When the great artists wish to picture the presence of God Himself, it is by painting a white dove that they show it!"

Carlo stood for a moment, almost unbelieving. The bird, so delicate and pure, turned her tiny head in his direction. Suddenly the sunlight blazed like a holy fire. The statue, the square, the golden walls and roof tops, took on a heavenly beauty. For Carlo, the humble friar who had gone into the fields and blessed the birds was no longer only a legend. He was a living spirit, bringing joy and peace to every gentle heart.

Carlo turned to Antonio with wonder in his eyes. "Maestro Doni was right," he said, half to himself. "And the Signora's prayers—they have been answered, after all. For the joy of Saint Francis is the joy of heaven itself. And there is nothing to compare with it in all the world."